Lisette's Angel

Amy Littlesugar

paintings by Max Ginsburg

Dial Books for Young Readers

NEW YORK

Published by Dial Books for Young Readers

A division of Penguin Putnam Inc. • 345 Hudson Street • New York, New York 10014

Text copyright © 2002 by Amy Littlesugar

Paintings copyright © 2002 by Max Ginsburg

All rights reserved • Designed by Nancy R. Leo-Kelly

Text set in Berthold Baskerville • Printed in Hong Kong on acid-free paper

1 3 5 7 9 10 8 6 4 2

Library of Congress Cataloging-in-Publication Data

Littlesugar, Amy. Lisette's angel/by Amy Littlesugar ; paintings by Max Ginsburg.

p.   cm.

Summary: In World War II France, a young girl prays for an angel to rescue her from the Nazi invasion.

ISBN 0-8037-2435-7

1. World war, 1939–1945–France–Juvenile fiction. 2. France–History–German occupation, 1940–1945–Juvenile fiction.

[1. World War, 1939–1945–France–Fiction. 2. France–History–German occupation, 1940–1945–Fiction].

I. Ginsburg, Max, ill. II. Title.

PZ7.L7362 Li 2002   [E]–dc21   99-087549

The full-color artwork was prepared using oil paints.

❖ ❖ ❖

Author's Note

During World War II (1939–1945), the French people endured German occupation for over four years. In the fall of 1943, secret radio messages from London began to hint at an invasion by American and British troops. But how and where?

Along the northern coast of France, in the region of Normandy, the Germans had built up a wall of concrete, steel, and deadly explosives. Surely Allied troops would not risk landing there. Yet in the moonlit hours of June 6, 1944, more than seventeen thousand paratroopers did land–catching most German soldiers off guard.

But many paratroopers were blown off course, some drowning in marshes flooded by Germans, while others, luckier, landed in gardens like Lisette and Emile's. French people young and old risked their lives rescuing these "angels from the sky."

This story was inspired by the memories of my father-in-law, who was a paratrooper. One remembrance that especially touched him were the ragged yet brave French children of a badly bombed-out village. He gave away his entire ration of Hershey's bars, while a buddy gave up his government-issued silk chute, which he knew would make someone a new dress or suit.

Several years ago, on the anniversary of D-day, I put on my father-in-law's silver jump wings and journeyed to Normandy. And there, with the help of many French friends who had memories of their own, I wrote *Lisette's Angel*.

W HEN I WAS A GIRL, I lived in a beautiful land called Normandy on the windy coast of northern France. There apple trees grew near the sea, and brown-and-white cows gave the sweetest milk.

Ma puce—my flea—Maman and Papa called me and my little brother, Emile. For they loved us very much, and we were happy.

One day Maman fitted me for a brand-new dress. It had pink roses on it, and dancing butterflies. She made a collar of lace as delicate as two snowflakes.

I'd walk with my toes pointed and my chin up whenever I wore it.

Then, when I was six, German soldiers in gray uniforms came.

"Click-clack! Click-clack!" went their black boots, echoing along the cobblestones.

They hung a bloodred flag in the village square. They staked barbed wire along the beach. And in the fields where the poppies grew, tanks with big guns pierced the sky.

No one was happy anymore. When we went into Monsieur Lomoine's shop in the village, it was almost always empty. No sugar. No coffee. No soap. The German soldiers had taken everything for themselves.

This was hard for Emile to understand. He longed for the chocolates Monsieur Lomoine had kept in a tall glass case. The ones in silver-and-brown paper.

"Maman," he'd beg, "can't I have just one chocolate? Please?"

Maman would kneel down, for there were soldiers everywhere, and remind him very quietly, "There is a war on, *ma puce*. You know that. Chocolate is for the soldiers."

One day Maman noticed how much I'd grown, how small my beautiful dress had become. But in Monsieur Lomoine's shop there wasn't a scrap of cloth to be found . . . not a button or a pin.

The roses and dancing butterflies had faded. The lace collar like two snowflakes was ragged and frayed.

Maman let out all the seams and lowered the hem.

"Your dress must last until the war is over, Lisette," she said sadly. "If that day ever comes."

Some nights, long after Emile was asleep, I'd go to our window and look up into the stars.

"For every star," my grandmother used to say, "there is an angel."

"Mon Dieu"—Dear God—I'd whisper. "Please help us. Please send us an angel."

Then, when I was nine, coded messages were sent over the radio to the people of France almost every night. The German soldiers had forbidden us to listen and demanded that people give up their radios, but we hid ours and listened anyway. The messages said that thousands of ships and planes would soon come across the sea to save us.

"BE BRAVE, MY FRIENDS," the radio voice told us. "DO NOT GIVE UP HOPE."

But days and weeks went by and no ships came. No planes either.

And soon it was winter, and our coal was all gone. Our flour too. Maman scraped the cellar floor for sawdust to make our bread.

Emile no longer asked for chocolate.

And I stopped praying for an angel to come.

❖ ❖ ❖

One terrible day Monsieur Lomoine was arrested. Little by little he'd been putting things aside for his friends and neighbors. Sugar for old Madame Benet. Cake for the orphans in the village. Soap for the Maurais family, whose papa was ill and could not work. The soldiers laid out all the things on the street for us to see.

There was chocolate in silver-and-brown paper, and the prettiest cloth— like a summer garden. But none of this mattered anymore. Monsieur Lomoine was our friend.

"We must help him, Papa!" I cried.
"Tais-toi"—Hush!—Papa whispered. "There's nothing we can do."

That night I looked up into a gray and starless sky. Where were the ships and the planes? Where was our angel?

And with only the moon to hear, I cried myself to sleep.

It was Emile who heard them first, roaring out of the clouds.

"Lisette. Lisette!"

I woke up. Now I heard them too. I ran to the window and stood beside him.

There, spread out across the moonlit sky, wing touching wing, were the planes.

"Look at all the stars!" Emile cried. They seemed to fill the sky.

And then I saw it. *Mon Dieu,* I saw it! An angel—falling from the sky!

Down, down it came, a big fluttering shadow, as big as Maman's garden. When it hit the ground, we heard a thud, then a groan. And at the same time, another sound.

Click-clack! Click-clack! The sound of the soldiers' boots.

Emile's cold fingers gripped my wrist. "We must get Papa, Lisette."

But Papa and Maman had gone to sit with poor Monsieur Maurais.

Click-clack! Click-clack!

"Come on," I said, grabbing Emile's hand.

The angel lay very still in the silver grass.

"Is he dead?" Emile asked.

At that, the angel sat up.

"American," he said, pointing to the little flag at his shoulder. Then he pulled a small knife from his pocket, cut himself free from the star, and struggled to stand.

He was the tallest angel there ever was. But he was hurt. I saw that right
away. And without any words, I went up to him and took his hand.
   Click-clack! Click-clack!
   We stumbled toward the barn, Emile trying to help, but slipping twice
in the long, wet grass.

Inside, the angel knelt down in the straw beside the cows. Farine, oldest and wisest, lowed gently. She knew he was an angel too.

Then Emile looked at me.

"Lisette," he whispered. "We forgot the star!"

I turned and looked out the barn door. The star lay where we'd left it, sparkling and shimmering, all over Maman's leeks and poppies.

The German soldiers would see it at once.

I raced back and tried to grab hold of it.

"Whoosh!" it whispered, like moonlight that would not be caught.

CLICK-CLACK!! CLICK-CLACK!! The soldiers were here!

"Hurry, Lisette!" Emile called. "Hurry!"

My heart hammered in my chest. My arms and legs burned like fire. The barn felt as far away as a dream.

But I would not give up.

And none too soon, "You made it, Lisette!" Emile whispered. Close at last.

Then we shut the door and waited for the boot steps that came and stopped.

No one moved.

No one spoke.

No one breathed. Not for the longest, longest time.

The soldiers were talking right outside the barn.

One laughed roughly, and Emile shivered.

I clutched the star to me, silky soft. Warm and white.

And then, just as quickly as they'd come, the boot steps turned and clattered away.

"They'll be back," the angel said. Although we did not speak English, we understood.

He was on his feet now, fumbling in those great big pockets.

"Here, kid," he said, tossing something to Emile. Something in silver-and-brown paper.

"Chocolate! Look, Lisette." Emile's eyes were shining. "It's chocolate!"

"*Merci,* monsieur," I said, and the angel smiled down at me.

"No," he said softly. "Thank you."

And I understood that too.

Then, our angel was gone.

Suddenly I remembered the star. I ran after him, but he'd already disappeared into the shadows.

"I think he wanted you to have it, Lisette," said Emile.

The night sky was bright with soldier fire now. The church bells were ringing, and everywhere we looked, more and more stars were drifting toward earth.

Maman and Papa would find us soon. They'd cover us with kisses and hold us tight.

Then we'd tell about our angel. About the silver-and-brown paper Emile would save forever, and the star—the sparkling, shimmering star.

One day Maman would snip it and sew it into a beautiful surprise just for me.

"Whoosh," it would whisper when I walked once more with my toes pointed and my chin up.

Once more in a beautiful land—where there are no bloodred flags or barbed wire near the beach—where apple trees grow near the sea, and where brown-and-white cows give the sweetest milk.